CONTENTS

Chapter		Page
1.	Annabelle's Friend—That's Me!	1
2.	Letter from a V.I.P.	11
3.	The Spelldown	18
4.	The Joy of Giving	26
5.	Really a Hero!	34
6.	United We Stand!	42
7.	The Birds Take Over	51
8.	The Very Queer Ball Game	58
9.	Dishpan Hands	66
10.	Pertunias and Onions	75
11.	A Fishing Trip	83

For

My Mother

DOUBLE TROUBLE for Rupert

By ETHELYN M. PARKINSON

Illustrated by Mary Stevens

SCHOLASTIC BOOK SERVICES

NEW YORK • TORONTO • LONDON • AUCKLAND • SYDNEY

Copyright 1953, 1954, 1955, 1956, 1957, 1958 by W. L. Jenkins. Copyright © 1958 by TAB Books, Inc. Published by Scholastic Book Services, a division of Scholastic Magazines, Inc.

11th printing..............................January 1971

Printed in the U.S.A.

Annabelle's Friend—That's Me!

WAKEFIELD is a keen town and I, Rupert Piper, and the guys have a swell time, usually. The girls are a trial, and sometimes they scandalize us. But all in all, we wouldn't trade Wakefield for San Francisco, or New York.

Even Lincoln School has its good points, if you don't count too high. The sixth grade is the best grade, and our teacher, Miss Carlman, is keen. We spend a lot of time in school, and it's certainly no man's world there! We guys have one small corner in the schoolyard

1

which belongs to us and to us alone, and that is the "No Dames" corner. The girls can stand around and listen, but they cannot come in. This much respect they show us.

Well, like I said, we spend a lot of time in school and today was no exception. Simply because I ate ten wheat cakes for breakfast, which made me a little late, Milt Morrissey left for school without me! You'd think Milt would know that a guy has to eat a big breakfast to be able to last through a hard day at school.

So I wheeled off to school by my lonesome. And just in time, too. I edged down in my seat as the second bell rang. Milt winked at me, so I winked back. Like I said, the guys have to stick together.

I looked past Opal Duncan's pigtails and saw Miss Carlman poke her glasses up on her nose in a certain way. That always means bad news for the sixth grade. The minute she put her glasses on that morning, Clayton Snow poked me and said, "Something's up, Piper!"

"Clayton Snow and Rupert Piper—quiet!" said Miss Carlman.

She waited until all was still. "We will *not* sing!" she announced in the voice of doom.

"Oh-Oh!" murmured Milt. Milt's very musical. That is, he can't sing a tune but he's the *loudest* singer in sixth.

Trowbridge "Doodleberries" Hall grinned from ear to big red ear. Miss Carlman looked at him, and he wiped the grin off—but fast—and tried to look sad.

Miss Carlman went on. "Miss Rockletter and I had a

conference in her office. We have decided there is far too much quarreling on the school ground."

Smart Annabelle Willman raised her hand.

"Yes, Annabelle?"

"There were two fights yesterday, Miss Carlman," Annabelle reported. "There was one between Clayton . . ."

"Not now, Annabelle!" said Miss Carlman. "Anyway, I'm sure we'll all be glad to do something that will encourage friendship in the class—something that will make us kinder to each other and also help us make better use of our time."

Miss Carlman took off her glasses and smiled. "How many have ever heard of secret friends?"

No one had. Sometimes I think I have some secret enemies.

"Well," said Miss Carlman, "within five minutes everyone is going to have a secret friend. Annabelle and Trowbridge, will you pass these slips of paper?"

Doodleberries came down my row.

"Everyone write your name on your slip of paper and fold it," instructed Miss Carlman. "Now, pass the slips forward for Annabelle and Trowbridge to collect."

Smart Annabelle juggled the slips, but Doodleberries kept an eagle eye on her.

"Now the slips will be passed around," Miss Carlman said. "Take one, and don't let anyone else see it."

Annabelle passed me a slip. I waited till she slow-poked past me, then I peeked. Sure enough, I had Annabelle's name.

"The name you've drawn is the name of the person to whom you are to be a secret friend," Miss Carlman said. "That means you must do some helpful thing for that person every day, if possible, without letting him or her guess that you're a secret friend."

Talk about being on a spot! That meant I had to think up some beautiful thing to do for Smart Annabelle every day. I never did anything to deserve that!

I cheered up when I thought of getting a very playful little garter snake to put in Annabelle's lunch box for a pet. She would never know whom to thank. But it would teach her to love snakes.

"Now, starting with Trowbridge," Miss Carlman said, "please bring your slips to me, one at a time, so I'll have a record of secret friends."

Trapped! There's always a catch. I decided Annabelle wouldn't appreciate a snake.

"Now," said Miss Carlman, when she'd signed away our freedom, "while you're doing nice things for the person whose name you've drawn, your own secret friend will be doing nice things for you. And, remember, anyone may be your secret friend, so it will pay to be nice and friendly to everyone!"

Annabelle raised her hand. "Miss Carlman, when will we know our secret friends?"

"In about a month." Miss Carlman smiled. "This week, you are to give your friend a very small gift. When you receive your gift from your secret friend, you are to make the most of it. That means, get just as much good out of it as you can. When the month

is over, the boy or girl who made the best use of his
gift will win a prize."

On the way home, Doodleberries said, "I hope I'll
get something to eat for my gift. There's one sure way
to get the most good out of something to eat."

A truck passed us. On it was a big sign:

SAY IT WITH FLOWERS.

"I wish it was summer," I said. "Our lawn would
probably be covered with hundreds of beautiful yellow flowers. Namely, dandelions!"

Clayte snickered. "Ours too! There are lots of beautiful gifts of nature in summer. But this is fall."

I went home and looked at my rock collection. I
guessed I'd give Smart Annabelle an agate and let her
use her wonderful brains to figure how to get the most
good out of it.

I went out to the kitchen. Mother's egg lady had
been there. The eggs were in the basket on the table.
I noticed one egg was bigger than the rest. In fact
it was *some* egg.

"I'd like to see the tough old hen that laid that egg,"
I said.

Next I thought of Annabelle. There is just one thing
you can do with an egg. I could hear Annabelle saying, "My gift was an egg. I ate it."

That would get a laugh.

There was a lot of mystery that week. I saw Clayte
buying peanuts, but he never offered me one. Opal
asked me what kind of Kodak Doodleberries had.

On Friday, all the gifts were turned in to Miss Carlman. We opened them just before dismissal.

Doodleberries got a roll of film. Clayte got a book. He groaned. "There's only one thing you can do with a book. Use it for a doorstop."

"You can sell it for scrap paper and use the money to buy something to eat," Milt said.

Smart Annabelle tossed her head. "*Some* people *read* books," she said.

I opened my gift. It was a flower bulb.

"Oh, Rupert!" sighed Annabelle. "It will be so easy to make the most of that! Your secret friend must like you a lot, Rupert!"

I looked out the window.

At last it was Annabelle's turn. She opened her package and peeked.

"We-ell!" she said. "We-ell!"

"My goodness," said Opal through her nose, "It's an egg!"

Everyone—except the guys—felt sorry for Annabelle.

"Some people use eggs for shampoos," said Beautiful Sylvia Singer, as if anyone had asked her.

"And some people save the shells and make darling little Easter dolls," said Mary Chandler.

"Some people boil 'em and eat 'em," said Clayte.

"H'm," said Annabelle. "Thank you, secret friend, whoever you are!"

On the way home, Doodleberries asked me, "Piper, what are you going to do with your beautiful flower bulb?"

"Nothing. If it fits my Kodak, I might take it up to Bear Paw Camp next summer."

"How about the book, Clayte?"

"I'm going to donate it to the school library." Clayte grinned.

Milt came up. "Guys," he said, "did you hear about the prize? It's a double aquarium, with your choice of turtles or fish—but it's to be kept in our room."

"H'm," I said. "A girl would certainly choose fish, but we guys want turtles, so a guy *has* to win."

"Now, you're talking," Clayte agreed. "I'll be very busy reading tonight!"

I went home and looked at the bulb again. There was a slip stapled to it that told how to plant it.

Mother loaned me a heavy green glass dish. I got some little stones from the driveway and put them in the dish. I put the bulb in the middle and covered it with water.

I'll admit the sixth grade was too busy to fight. I found things like cookies in my pockets. And I'm no slouch or cheapskate. I put some gum in Annabelle's desk, and even bought her a cone. She was very happy and asked after the health of my flower bulb.

"It's got a bud," I said. "Was your egg good?"

Annabelle laughed. "Oh, *very* good, Rupert!"

The day came. Everyone went to school carrying very queer-looking packages which were turned over to Miss Carlman.

At three o'clock we had our program. "We're going to tell how we made the most of our secret friends' gifts," Miss Carlman announced. "Then we'll vote for the prize winner."

I could hardly wait for the big moment to come when Annabelle would stand up and say: "I received an egg. I boiled it and ate it." What a laugh for the guys!

Beautiful Sylvia got up first. "I received a yard of printed cotton," she said. "I wanted to put it to some use that would be both pretty and practical, so I made this little apron."

She fastened the apron around herself, and the girls all clapped very loud. Of course, it wasn't a good carpenter apron. It left the guys cold.

Mary was next. "I received a bag of peanuts," she said. Clayte turned red as a tomato. "Of course,"

Mary said, "I could have eaten them, or I could have made some squirrel very happy. But instead I made these peanut cookies and I'm going to pass them around."

The cookies were good but pretty small. The guys clapped—some.

Doodleberries got up. "I received a roll of film," he said. "I went down to the Capitol one Saturday, and I got some pictures of the buildings we've studied about. I'll pass them around."

The guys clapped very loud. It would be hard to beat Doodleberries by eating an egg.

Clayte had read his book and loaned it to the library. Fifteen other people gave their reports. Then it was my turn.

"I received a flower bulb," I said. "I planted it, and I have here a beautiful narcissus for all the class to enjoy."

I noticed Smart Annabelle was clapping louder than some of the guys.

At last it was her turn. She drifted up to the front and smiled like some actress.

"My dear secret friend gave me an egg," she said. "Since I don't use egg shampoos, eating it seemed to be the only thing to do. And then I got to thinking. What really is the most good that can be gotten out of an egg? And suddenly I knew. So . . ."

She stepped out into the hall and returned with a little wire cage. In it was a funny little peeping "critter." I guess my eyes popped.

"I read in Clayte's book how to make a home incubator," Annabelle said. "And I hatched this little turkey. I'm going to keep it a while. Then my farmer-uncle is going to take over. And—well, we're sure of turkey, not *this* Thanksgiving but *next* Thanksgiving!"

You should have heard the girls clap.

Not the guys!

Poor Miss Carlman reached for her glasses.

I leaned over and whispered to Annabelle, "If you win the aquarium, will you choose fish or turtles?"

"Turtles," said Annabelle. I told you she was smart. She had certainly hatched a fine turkey from my turkey egg!

When I started clapping, all the guys joined in, and you never heard better noise.

Miss Carlman laid her glasses down and asked, "Then —does Annabelle get first prize?"

Everyone voted "yes." But the one who voted loudest was Annabelle's secret friend—that's me!

Letter from a V. I. P.

WE WERE down in the "No Dames" corner having a very important discussion about the turtle aquarium when the second bell rang, and were we disgusted!

Doodleberries looked at his watch. "Miss Rockletter's clock is two seconds fast again," he said.

We were the last ones into the sixth-grade room. "As usual!" cracked Beautiful Sylvia.

Miss Carlman had her arms crossed and her eyes on her watch. She's plenty keen but she sure doesn't

11

care how much she overworks a guy. She plunged right
in about our letter writing.

"Some people do not seem to be interested in learning to write a correct letter," she told us. "Will someone tell me why this is?"

Clayte poked me. "Keep out of it, Piper. Anything
you say will be used against you."

"Clayton Snow and Rupert Piper—quiet!" said Miss
Carlman. "Milton, I think you raised your hand before Annabelle did."

Milt stood up and gave Smart Annabelle a big bow.
"After you, fair lady!" he said.

"Why, thank you!" said Annabelle. "Miss Carlman, I
think girls are naturally more interested in writing letters. But if the boys had someone very interesting to
write to, maybe they would enjoy it."

Annabelle sat down, and it was old Milt's turn.
"Miss Carlman," he said, "these are very modern times.
And the guys—I mean the boys—are going to be very
modern businessmen. We will use telegrams and tele-
phones and cablegrams. And if it is necessary to write
letters, we will have our secretaries write them. Thank
you." Milt sat down.

Miss Carlman looked very astonished. "Well!" she
said. "Well! Mister Morrissey, has no one ever told
you that a businessman dictates letters to his secretary?"

Beautiful Sylvia waved. "Miss Carlman, I have just
thought of something."

"Oh-Oh!" Clayte moaned.

"It would be fun," Sylvia said, "for each of us to write

a letter to some V.I.P. That means Very Important Person, in case someone does not know."

Doodleberries waved. "Miss Carlman, we have nothing to say in a letter. We do not have any important news. We live in a very small town, and the things we know about, such as arithmetic and spelling, are not interesting to an important person."

Smart Annabelle waved. "Miss Carlman, wouldn't it be fun to ask the V.I.P. what was the greatest thrill of his life and ask him to please answer."

"That," said Miss Carlman, "is a fine idea, because the V.I.P. will not answer a poor letter."

So that was that.

"Dad," I said at supper, "do you believe in writing letters?"

"Depends," Dad said. "Please pass the sugar, Rupert."

Mom spoke up. "Rupert, why are you interested in letters?"

"I am not," I said. "But Miss Carlman is. I have to coax some V.I.P. to write to me. Do we know any V.I.P.?"

"Certainly," Dad said. "I have met two top baseball stars."

"We know Uncle John Coldwell," Mom said. "Rupert, you haven't seen him since you were three. He is your daddy's uncle."

My sister Gwen said, "He is a writer. He has traveled all over the world."

"He was born in this town," said Dad, "and he went to Lincoln School."

"That was no thrill," I said. "Where does Uncle John live now?"

"In New York," Gwen said.

"I have his address," Mom told me. "You may write to him tonight."

"What can I tell him?" I wondered. "This is a slow, horse-and-buggy town. I never do anything."

"You play ball, and swim, and fish," Mom said. "You take piano lessons, and collect rocks, and take pictures, and print them."

"Very thrilling." I moaned. "I am sure Uncle John will want to meet a guy who does such wonderful things."

Well, I did not know any other V.I.P., so I wrote to Uncle John Coldwell. What else could I do?

Dear Uncle John:

I am Rupert Piper and I think you remember my dad. I am eleven and I go to Lincoln School.

This town is still a small town. There is a creek called Swedetown Creek where we go fishing. It is very small and almost dried up in August. You can walk out on the rocks, and little turtles sit there and blink at you. Little birds flit around, and many little birds and bugs keep singing. This is all we do for excitement.

Please write and tell me the most thrilling thing that ever happened to you.

Love from your great-nephew.

Rupert

I went out to mail my letter. Then I went home and looked in our bookcase. There were some books by

John Coldwell. I was very surprised to find he had had many thrilling adventures. He was attacked by a tiger in Africa. He had to bail out over mountains in Italy. He was really a V.I.P. Now if he would only write me about one of his adventures!

All the guys and girls were very jittery, waiting for their letters. Opal's arrived first, but it was signed by a secretary. Doodleberries received a good letter from a ranger—all about fighting a forest fire.

But when my letter came, I almost died three times. It said:

Dear Rupert:

Your letter made me very happy. It took me back, in memory, to the most thrilling day of my life—the day I caught my first brook trout in Swedetown Creek.

I was only eight years old. I had saved ten cents to buy a fishing outfit. I had a new line—I still remember the newness of it. I had black steel hooks, five different sizes, in a white box. I had a cork bobber and three sinkers. I had bought them weeks before and I had looked at them every day.

And now the day had come, and I was going fishing with my dad and brother. I remember the two-mile walk to the creek. The snow had melted and the smell of spring was in the air. The May flowers were blooming. The crows cawed over our heads. Everything looked so new—the woods, the fields, even the sky.

When we reached the creek, we cut some willow poles. I cut my line, tied on my bobber, sinker, and hook. I put down my line and waited.

I remember how it was. The first song sparrows were singing. The cowslips were yellow at my feet. All around me I could hear faint sounds from the ground and bushes and trees, and from all the earth things that were coming to life.

Suddenly my bobber dipped, and I felt a pull. How my heart pounded! I jerked my rod upward, and there at the end of my new line gleamed that beautiful fish! My heart still beats fast when I remember. And here, in my city house, I can close my eyes and see the woods and streams, and I can hear the sounds—and smell the smells of spring on Swedetown Creek.

There is nothing like it here in the city, Rupert. And I had never known a greater thrill, a happier day, than the one I spent catching a fish in Swedetown Creek.

Your Uncle John

So that was my letter from a V.I.P., and I guessed it was a flop. I guessed Uncle John did his best but I should have written to some baseball player. We read the letters at a P.T.A. program. Opal read a letter written by some queen's secretary. She said the queen's greatest thrill was having the crown put on her head. Milt's was from a famous Western actor who told about seeing himself in his first movie.

But everybody's letter was more thrilling than mine, I guessed.

Miss Carlman called on me last, and I stood up to read. "Mine is from John Coldwell," I said. "He is a writer."

So I read, and something funny happened. All the dads stopped squirming in those little chairs. They all leaned forward and listened.

When I was through, they clapped and clapped, and while they were still clapping I saw a tall, gray-haired man standing in the doorway. Miss Smithwick said, "Why, Johnny Coldwell!"

Uncle John Coldwell came up and shook hands with Miss Carlman and put his arm around me.

He said, "Rupert wrote me a letter that made me want to come home. I'm on my way to Chicago to give a talk about some of my adventures. Do you care for a preview?"

"Do we!" said Milt's dad, and all the dads clapped.

So my V.I.P. gave a very thrilling speech—all about how he was chased by elephants and how he was captured once by a savage tribe, and how he was almost caught by a python.

Don Horne took his picture for the *Wakefield Gazette*.

"We'd better pose Rupert, too," said my Uncle John, "since it was his fine letter that brought me home."

I am a very honest guy. I said, "Miss Carlman taught me to write letters."

"Miss Carlman," said Uncle John, "will you do us the honor?"

So there we were in the *Gazette*—Miss Carlman and Uncle John Coldwell, and me, Rupert Piper.

The Spelldown

RUPERT PIPER!" said my mom in a very cold voice. "I've asked you three times to take these *Gazettes*, with your smiling face on the front page, out to the garage."

This voice I recognize and respect. "Sure, Mom, gladly will I leave my lunch of a hard-boiled egg, a glass of ice-cold milk, and a simply delectable salami-and-pickle sandwich long enough to do this job."

I put the *Gazettes* on top of the other papers. As I came out of the garage, Dood and Milt came up the driveway.

18

"Hurry, Piper, we'll be late for school," Dood said.

So I rushed into the kitchen, drank my milk, and ran out with the salami-and-pickle sandwich in my hand.

Dood said, "I have a strong feeling that we're going to catch it this afternoon."

Milt moaned. "All the girls got 100 in spelling this morning. I have a *very* strange feeling."

"And the guys all failed," I said. "It will be a sad afternoon."

We were right. As soon as the second bell rang, Miss Carlman pushed her glasses up on her nose and folded her arms.

"The girls did very well in spelling this morning," she said. "But every boy failed. When every boy in the Lincoln School sixth grade fails in spelling, something will have to be done."

Doodleberries groaned a little. Maybe I did, too.

"I could send some notes home to parents," Miss Carlman said. "Unless someone has a suggestion."

Clayte and I put up our hands. So did Milt and Dood.

"Miss Carlman," I said, "we could all put in some extra hours slaving—I mean studying."

"Annabelle's hand was raised first," Miss Carlman said. "Yes, Annabelle?"

"Miss Carlman," she said. "Couldn't we have a spell-down at the next P.T.A. meeting? If we were going to spell before our parents, we would all do our very best."

Beautiful Sylvia was waving her hand. She looked

very smarty-smart. Very! "Miss Carlman, wouldn't it be wonderful fun to spell against our fathers and mothers and see who wins?"

Miss Carlman smiled, "Lincoln School sixth grade against Lincoln School parents. It seems a very good idea, doesn't it, boys?"

Dood said, "It's very corny."

Miss Carlman frowned a special frown at Dood.

The fellows met down in the "No Dames" corner to talk it over. "We've got to decide," I said, "what we're going to do about the spelldown."

"We can take care of it all if we write a very smart invitation to our parents," Milt said. "Rupert, you got a pencil and paper?"

I took my trusty Ever-Go and a chocolate-bar wrapper from my pocket.

"Take a letter," Milt said.

He dictated. "Dear Mom and Dad, You are cordially invited . . ."

"How do you spell 'cordially'?" I asked.

"C-o-r-d- Put that much down and we'll look it up later," Milt said. "You are cordially invited to participate . . ."

"Spelling!" I said.

"P-a-r-t- We'll look it up."

Well the letter looked this way when I finished it:

Dear Mom and Dad, You are cord—invitted to part— in a spelldown between the sixth grade and there parrents. Some of the sixth grade are very good spelers, and always get one hundred, because they can spell all the jaw-

brakers in the speling book. You will reely have to be
good, to spell them down. We will see wich side wins.
Of course you will never live it down if some sixth grade
girl or boy is a better speler than you, so we are in-
vitting you in pleanty of time so that you can get a
speling book and reely studdy it until middnight every
night. Your lovving son, who is a verry bright speling
puppil . . .

"There!" Milt said. "That ought to scare them."

Dood looked it over. "There's a word spelled wrong,"
he said. "'Pupil' is spelled wrong."

"We'd better look up all the words," I said. "I wasn't
sure of a lot of them."

So we looked up every word and then we wrote our
letters.

The next day we had very sad news. "My folks took
the dare," Dood groaned unhappily.

"So did mine," said Clayte. "I've got to bring home
a spelling book so Dad can bone up."

"Some keen idea I had," Milt said. "Some keen idea!
What do we do now?"

I felt very sad. "I hate to say it," I said. "I hate to
break the news. We have to study."

"We can study at my house," Milt said.

"Oh, no," Clayte said. "This isn't going to be any TV
studying. We'd better study in our garage." The guys
studied in Clayte's garage that night. We spelled out
loud and didn't eat our cookies and sandwiches until
everyone knew the first three pages.

"Know something?" Milt said while we were eating,

"Annabelle can spell in class, but she can't spell in a letter. I saw some notes she wrote to Sylvia."

"Sylvia wrote a note to my sister Gwen," I said. "She spelled 'coming' wrong. She spelled it right in class and she spelled it wrong in a letter the very next day. So if the girls don't review, they might forget words, too."

Tuesday morning Annabelle asked me, "Where were you last night, Rupert?"

"Oh, around," I said.

"You weren't playing ball," Sylvia said. "And you weren't swimming. Where were you?"

"I was very busy studying," I said. In my mind I spelled "studying" with one "d".

"Oh, no, you weren't!" said Opal. "We went past your house and you weren't at your desk."

I was wondering how I could get away from the girls when I heard someone calling me. "Hey, Rupert! Scram over here!"

It was Police Chief Fox over in front of the City Hall. I ran across the street to see what he wanted.

"Rupert," he said, "about that spelldown. You tell Miss Carlman—wait, I'll give you a note."

He took a pencil from his pocket, and then a piece of paper, and then a book to write on. I've got eyes. The book was a sixth-grade spelling book.

So Chief Fox wrote a note. "There!" he said. "You take that along, Rupert."

I never meant to read the note, but it was wide open and I've got eyes.

The note said: "Dear Miss Carlman, Don't you worry

about the P.T.A. food. I got a fine donation. I'll bring enough beef barbycue to feed the whole town. . . ."

I was astonished, appalled, and chagrined. The first word on page ten of the spelling book was "barbecue," spelled "b-a-r-b-e-c-u-e."

I delivered the note, then got my spelling book to check. Chief Fox was wrong. While I was checking, I felt someone looking over my shoulder. It was Miss Carlman and she gave me a very funny little smile.

The spelldown was Thursday night. The sixth grade stood on one side of the room and the parents stood on the other side. Milt's uncle stood between and gave out the words.

The parents had lots of fun, but they couldn't spell very well. Clayte's dad went down on "judgment" and Clayte spelled it right.

"You wait till I get you home!" Clayte's dad said.

Then my mom got "seize." My mom is very smart and went to college, but she spelled "seize" wrong. She spelled it "s-e-e-z-e," and then she said, "Oh, no," and blushed and laughed and looked real pretty, but corrections were not allowed.

Opal spelled "seize" through her nose, and you should have seen Dad laugh at Mom.

Then the dads began going down like bowling pins. Milt's dad went down on "perseverance." Smart Annabelle went down on the same word. When Milt's uncle said, "Wrong!", Annabelle looked very surprised and sat down quick.

Miss Smithwick went down on the same word, and I was next. The word was in the second row on page seventeen. I could close my eyes and see it. I spelled it.

"Right!" said Milt's uncle.

Annabelle wiped her eyes and stared at me.

The words got harder and everybody was going down. The parents went down one by one, and the girls went down, and after a while Clayte and Dood

got excited and went down on "subpoena." Chief Fox spelled it right.

Then Sylvia went down on "knead"—to knead bread —and Chief Fox spelled it right. There was no one left but Chief Fox and me!

We spelled and spelled, winking across at each other. I'll never forget it. My knees felt like rubber, and my heart was whacking. The guys were rooting for me, and the dads were rooting for Chief Fox, and my mom was looking proud enough to burst.

And then it happened. Chief Fox got "barbecue." The poor guy!

He spelled it just the way he did in the note. "B-a-r-b-y-c-u-e."

"Wrong!" said Milt's uncle.

I shook. I took a big breath and looked away from Mom and spelled "barbecue."

"Right!" said Milt's uncle.

You should have seen Miss Carlman's face.

'Puff out your chest!" said Bill Horner, as my dad got ready to take the winner's and the runner-up's picture.

Chief Fox winked at me. He was as happy as if he had won. I winked back at him.

All the guys were clapping, and just as the bulb flashed, I looked at Miss Carlman. She looked happy, too, to think that a boy had won, and I felt wonderful.

The Joy of Giving

THANKSGIVING was just around the corner and everyone knows that a Thanksgiving basket is a very fine thing. When Miss Carlman asked us if we wished to buy one for some family, we all voted yes. It meant earning money, but the sixth grade is used to that! But earning it the way *we* did was never the guys' idea!

When something is worky, you can be sure that Smart Annabelle and Beautiful Sylvia dreamed it up! Those two would rather work than eat!

26

Miss Carlman folded her arms. She said, "I feel that your parents are having enough expense, and so it is not fair to ask them to pay for your Thanksgiving basket. Does anyone have a suggestion? Yes, Milton?"

Milt stood up. "We can give the money out of our allowance and never feel it," he said.

"We-ell," Miss Carlman said, "we really should feel it!"

Annabelle said, "I think it would be wrong to give allowance money since our parents provide that. We cannot know the joy of giving unless we work for the money ourselves." She smiled. Just talking about work makes Annabelle happy.

"Very true," said Miss Carlman. "Yes, Sylvia?"

Sylvia stood up. "Wouldn't it be fun to hire out to do odd jobs for ladies who need help?"

Annabelle waved again. "There is a bulletin board in Peterson's Grocery. All the mothers could have a 'Help Wanted' list, and we could read it, and then hire out on Saturday."

"A very good idea," said Miss Carlman.

Well, it did not look good to the guys. We hurried down to the "No Dames" corner to talk it over.

"A fine thing!" said Doodleberries. "I know how ladies work it. The ad will say, 'Wanted: Boy to run errands.' But does that mean to go to the grocery on your bicycle, which would be a man's work? Oh, no! That means to take a loaf of banana bread and a little glass of jelly to Grandma Duncan, twelve blocks away, and carry out her ashes."

"And it means to stop at Aunt Jane's for an apron

pattern," Doodleberries said. "And wait while Aunt
Jane feeds the baby, and wait again while she looks
in the attic and in the basement until she finds the
pattern."

Right then Milt had a keen idea. "If we don't go to
Peterson's Grocery," Milt said, "we won't see the list
and we won't have to work."

"Milt," Clayte said, "you are a genius. Washington,
D.C. needs men like you."

"Thank you, my friend, thank you," Milt said. He
made a deep, big bow, and while he was bent over, he
began to stare at the ground. So we bent over and
looked, too, and we saw what he saw.

"It's a ring!" I said, and Clayte grabbed it up.

It was a plain yellow ring with one white stone, and
it was all covered with mud.

"Dime-store ring," Milt said. "Let me see." He
wiped some of the mud on his pants.

"Let me see." Dood said.

We all decided it was a dime-store ring.

Saturday morning, I came downstairs ready to work.
"Give me my breakfast, Ma," I said, "and then I'll wash
the dishes."

"Oh, I wouldn't dream of asking you to do dishes,"
Ma said. "I wouldn't think of it."

She thought I would go right to Peterson's Grocery
and read the list and hire out as someone's chore-boy.
Not me! I was too smart a cooky.

I went over to Milt's. Clayte and Dood were there.
Their mothers had tried to get them to go to Peterson's, too.

So we just took it easy all morning. We went over to the sandlot and batted a few, and when it was noon, we started home.

We passed Mrs. Singmaster, sweeping her walk. She smiled at us. "I suppose you boys have lots to be thankful for."

"Oh, yes." I said.

"We're having a big turkey," Milt said.

"That's nice," said Mrs. Singmaster. "We're not having turkey this year, but Mr. Singmaster is well enough to walk, and Bill is better, too, so we're very thankful."

Mr. Singmaster got hurt at work, and Billy had polio.

"I guess we shouldn't beef," I said, as we went along.

"Mrs. Singmaster sure has had a hard time," Milt said.

"Turkey would be very good for Billy," said Clayte. "And that reminds me—I'm very hungry."

So was I. When I got home lunch was over, and I looked in our kitchen, and was I surprised!

Dishwater was splashing, and dishes were banging, and who do you suppose was standing at our sink, washing dishes and wasting a big smile on me, when she saw me? Annabelle!

"How come?" I said.

"Oh, I work here now!" Annabelle said. "I'm your mother's chore-girl. Didn't you see her ad in Peterson's Grocery this morning? 'Wanted: Eleven-year-old girl to help in house today.' Didn't you see it, Rupert?"

"Guess not." I said.

"That's funny!" said Annabelle. It was right on the bulletin board. What job did you take?"

"I did not come home to answer questions," I said. "I came home to dinner."

"Well, you are too late, Rupert," said a voice. It was Mom. "You are not going to make a lot of extra work for Annabelle," she said.

Annabelle flipped her eyelashes at me.

"I'll get my own lunch," I said.

"You certainly will," said Mom. "But not here in Annabelle's kitchen."

Annabelle's kitchen! How do you like that?

So I started to Peterson's Grocery to get myself some lunch, and I met Milt and Dood and Clayte.

"Guess what!" Milt said, in a voice of doom. "Beautiful Sylvia is scrubbing our kitchen. She wouldn't let me come into it."

"Rosemary Wood was on our front porch shaking rugs," Clayte said. "When she saw me, she yelled: 'If you come in here, you have to take those muddy shoes off!' I was going to walk right past her, but my mom said, 'Clayton, you heard Rosemary. You can't walk on her rugs in your shoes.' So I said, 'O.K., I won't walk on her rugs at all.'"

"Opal is tending my kid brother," Dood said, "She is reading 'Red Riding Hood' through her nose. They both told me I could not speak out loud as I would disturb them. I wish the wolf would eat Red this time."

We took our dimes to Peterson's Grocery, and as long as we were there, we looked over the list to see what jobs we were escaping from.

Mrs. Wood wanted an eleven-year-old boy to run errands.

Mrs. Willman wanted a boy, age eleven, to sweep her porch and walks.

Mrs. Duncan wanted some poor boy, age eleven, to slave in her basement.

Beautiful Sylvia's mother wanted a strong boy, about eleven, to go shopping with her.

There was something else. "Look!" Milt squeaked. "Read this!"

We thought we were dreaming when we read:

LOST—DIAMOND RING, NEAR LINCOLN SCHOOL. INITIALS M.S. REWARD! MISS MINERVA SMITHWICK

"Where is the ring? Who's got it?" Milt said. "Rupert, you had it last!"

"I did not!" I said. "You did!"

We went out to the back of the store and searched through our pockets.

Dood found the ring in his shirt. We wiped it some more, and we found the letters: "M.S."

So we took it to Miss Smithwick. Miss Smithwick's eyes were red, and poor old Dood's face was redder, because she gave him a big, dopey kiss on his cheek. Then she gave us ten dollars.

"It was my grandmother's ring," she said. "It was wearing thin, and I intended to take it to the jeweler. I must have flipped it out of my purse, when I took out a handkerchief."

So we were rich.

"We will not have to be chore-boys," Milt said. "We have enough money to buy a Thanksgiving basket and we will not have to soil our fingers."

When I went home, Annabelle was just finishing her chores, and Mom was getting her purse.

"Here is your money, Annabelle," she said. "I want to thank you for being such a good little helper. You did all the work that Gwen would have done, and I know that you could have spent your Saturday in some far more pleasant way."

"Oh, I just loved working for you, Mrs. Piper,"

Annabelle said. Because she just loves working. "You know," she said, "our basket will be given to the Singmaster family. Mr. Singmaster is better now, and he can enjoy eating."

Mom said, "When you go home you can rest, because I'm sure your mother has hired some nice eleven-year-old boy to do her chores."

They both wasted smiles on me.

I wished I was dead three times, because the Singmasters are keen people.

So I went over to Annabelle's to do the horrible, honest thing I had to do. On the way I met Milt. He seemed very busy. "Hi!" he said. He was carrying groceries toward Sylvia's house.

"Hi!" I said. I got busy, too, on Mrs. Willman's porch and walks.

I could see Clayte down the block near Rosemary Wood's house, and I saw Dood back of Opal's, carrying ashes. They all looked very busy and very honest.

On Monday, the guys all had chore-boy money to turn in, and we had Miss Smithwick's ten dollars, too.

But I will tell you a secret. We felt happiest about the chore-boy money.

Really a Hero!

IT WAS quite a chore getting up to go to school after the nice peaceful Christmas vacation. And, sure enough, the sixth grade was greeted with a problem on our very first tired day back!

"Boys and girls," Miss Carlman said, "we have to get some new pictures for the school hall. The ones out there are torn and yellowy dirty. Miss Rockletter thought that perhaps this class would have a good idea."

Milt waved. "Miss Carlman," he said, "I read a very educational article."

"We-ell!" Miss Carlman said.

Milt nodded. "This article was on decorating rooms and it said pictures should be chosen with great care. There's a baseball pitcher who's a very great hero, so if the fellows have the say . . ."

"The boys," Miss Carlman stated, "will not have all the say."

Sylvia waved. "Miss Carlman, Leonard Posey received a beautiful flash camera for his birthday. Maybe he could take classroom pictures, and take some outside of school, too. They would look good in the hall."

"An interesting idea," Miss Carlman said. "Leonard is absent with a cold, but I'll talk to him. Ready for recess!"

The fellows went down to the "No Dames" corner to talk things over.

"A fine thing!" said Doodleberries. "A fine thing—having Nosey Posey getting pictures of us. No telling what kind of pictures he'll take!"

Saturday evening, I was having a little after-dinner lunch on the davenport when Annabelle's mother came to see my Mom about some committee. She brought her sewing along.

"I'm making a dress for Annabelle," she said. She held it up. It was made of some pink stuff. "It's a surprise. I'd like to finish it this afternoon."

So Mom got her sewing and they talked and sewed.

"I'm ready to turn this hem," Mrs. Willman said. "I wonder just how much to turn up. It's quite a problem, without Annabelle—or someone who's just her height."

"I—wonder," Mom said.

They looked at me. I could feel some little cold goose-pimples getting stirred up on my backbone.

"Rupert, dear." That was Mom, using her special voice that means I am going to have to do some kind, terrible deed.

I stuffed my cupcake in my mouth and dived for the door, but Mom grabbed me.

"Rupert, dear," she said, "just slip this pretty dress on for a minute. I know you'd love to do Annabelle's mother a little favor."

I'd rather be dead three times.

"I feel very sick," I said. "I itch all over. Mom, you wouldn't want me to break out with measles in Annabelle's dress."

"Stand still, Rupert," Mom said.

Then they did it. Mom got a wrestler's hold on me, and Mrs. Willman pulled Annabelle's old dress over my head.

I was never so disgraced. I wished I was in the Foreign Legion.

But the worst was yet to come.

The doorbell rang. Mom went, and I heard a terrible voice saying, "Is Rupert busy?"

In walked Nosey Posey with his camera.

He smiled at me very sweetly. "Good evening," he said. "You're looking charming this evening."

I showed him my teeth so Mom would think I was smiling. "Who invited you?" I said.

"*Rupert!*" said Mom.

"I was passing by," said Leonard. "I saw you standing there looking glamorous, so I came in to compliment you." He was monkeying with his camera.

Mom brought some pins for Mrs. Willman. "Stand still, Rupert," Mom said.

Right then, the camera flashed in my eyes.

Leonard smiled at me. "Well, good-by, Beautiful," he said. "I'll see you in my dreams." He hurried out.

I knew what he was going to do. He was going to take the film to the drugstore, and he was going to have pictures of me in Annabelle's dress to show around, and I was going to die three times.

"Gangway!" I yelled. "I'm going!"

"Rupert!" Mom dived for me, but I got through the door.

I jumped off the porch and ran after Nosey. He heard me coming and ducked into the grocery drive. I ran down the other side, and scrambled over the hedge, and gained on him.

He dashed out into Gray Street and began to yell: "Help! Help! Murder!"

Mrs. Haverkorn was talking to Mrs. Pipgrass. "Why, see that girl chasing Leonard Posey!" Mrs. Haverkorn said. "My goodness, isn't that scandalous?"

Leonard ran down Hubbard and ducked across Pearl Street, and ran toward the river, howling for help.

Then he disappeared.

I thought fast. There was just one place to disappear. Leonard had climbed down the ladder into Mr. Peterson's boat that's always tied there.

Only tonight it wasn't there. I ran and peeked over. Sure enough, there was Nosey standing on the ladder below me. He was just one foot above the water, which was very shallow, but wet.

"O.K., chum. Hand up that camera," I said.

"It's mine!" he yelled.

"O.K.," I said. I sat down on the dock. "I hope you are very comfortable down there, pal, as you are going to stay there all night."

"Rupert Piper," Leonard howled, "you let me come up!"

"Nobody's stopping you," I said, with a very sweet smile. "Come on! I'll give you a hand."

"I'll tell my mother on you!" he yelled. "I'll tell Miss Carlman!"

"Come on up," I said, "and tell them."

So he began to howl "Help!" and who should come down but Police Chief Fox.

"What's going on here?" he said.

"Piper won't let me come up!" Leonard yelled.

Chief Fox laughed. "So it's you, Rupert! I thought some girl had chased some boy down there.

"I was doing a kind deed," I said, "when he walked into our house and took a picture of me. All I want is the film."

"That film belongs to my sister!" Leonard yelled.

"Rupert, hold my billy club," Chief Fox said. He reached in his pocket. There was a flash.

I turned around. "Hey!" I said. "Are you taking pictures too, Chief Fox?"

"Come on up, Leonard," Chief Fox said. "We'll go over to Haanen's and have our films developed. Put

your dress in my car and come along, Rupert. I got a good shot of you."

Behind a guy's back! And I thought Chief Fox was my friend. My heart broke.

Mr. Haanen developed the films and printed them. Leonard laughed very loud at his picture of me. "Boy, that will sure look cute in the album!"

"Mine, too," said Chief Fox. "Got a fine shot of you, Leonard—chased right into the river—by a girl!"

"A—girl?" Leonard squeaked. "Chief Fox, you know that's Rupert!"

"Looks like a girl to me!" Chief Fox said. He showed us the picture. There was Leonard, hanging onto the ladder, looking scared. On the dock was a girl with a club. That's how it looked.

"Pretty cute!" Chief Fox bragged. "I'd like about thirty prints. How many are you ordering, Leonard?"

Leonard looked kind of sick. "Well, it's really Rupert's picture, he said. "I guess I'll just give the film to Rupert."

"And the print," Chief Fox said. "Suppose you do that, right now."

So Leonard gave me both, and I tore them up.

"I changed my mind," Chief Fox said. "I won't have any pictures made—unless you really need some, Rupert." He winked at me.

"No, I won't need any," I said.

"That sounds like a bargain, gentlemen," Chief Fox said. "And now, how about a soda?"

When I went home, the welcoming committee was waiting—my Mom and Annabelle's.

"Rupert," Mom said, "where is Annabelle's dress?" She had a very funny look on her face.

"Right here," I said.

I told them all about it. "I had to settle things with Leonard," I said, "because this is Annabelle's dress. My face didn't show in Chief Fox's picture, and people would think it was Annabelle who had chased Leonard down the ladder and was standing over him with a club, and Annabelle would be very disgraced!"

There was a scratch on my arm from Haverkorn's hedge. I held it up and rubbed it.

"You poor boy!" Mrs. Willman said. "Getting wounded—for Annabelle! You're really a hero!" She winked at Mom.

"Well, in that case," Mom said, "there's one piece of pie left—hero!"

Leonard did take some keen pictures of our class and the other classes in the school. He also took outdoor pictures. They are now in the hall right by Miss Rockletter's office. But I still heave a deep sigh when I think what *might* have happened!

United We Stand!

I WAS trudging to school after a very poor—to my mind—lunch, and I was feeling very poor, too. We'd had a keen deep snow and the guys should be feeling in top condition, but the fifth-grade fellows battered down our snow fort during recess and defeated us in battle. So we had decided to meet in the "No Dames" corner five minutes before school began. We had to talk it over.

I was the last one there. It was a very pitiful thing to know that fellows like Clayte and Milt and Dood had retreated under fire, led by their gallant, fleet-running general, Rupert Piper!

"A fine thing!" Clayte said, as I stepped into the corner. "A very fine thing to be beaten by fifth-grade boys!"

"I wouldn't say that," said Dood. "The fifth grade guys only threw the balls, but who made them? The fifth-grade girls!"

"And who kept bringing them up just as fast as they were made?" asked Milt. "The fifth-grade girls. And where were the sixth-grade girls that should have been helping us?"

He meant Smart Annabelle and Beautiful Sylvia and Opal and some others.

"They are too nice to make snowballs this year," I said. "They are too snooty."

"They would not soil their mittens," said Clayte. "You are right. We were not beaten by guys. We were beaten by our own dear, dear sixth-grade girls!"

The bell rang and we ran in, and in a few minutes we were in trouble.

"As you know," Miss Carlman said, "our class has always been like a big happy family with everyone working together. The joy of one has been the joy of all. The problems of some have been the problems of all."

"Oh, oh," Clayte whispered. "Watch this, Piper!"

Miss Carlman smiled, and Annabelle kind of hitched in her seat.

Miss Carlman said, "In a big family, when someone needs help, the others all forget their own pleasures and offer to do something. This is what cooperation means. Our class is just the same."

I looked at Milt. He was looking very surprised. This was news to us. Because when we needed help at the snow fort, we certainly did not hear any offers.

Miss Carlman went on, "I am sure you all know of a motto which says, 'United we stand, divided we fall.' This is true of our class."

It is true of a snow battle, and that is why we fell.

Just then Miss Rockletter tapped on the door and Miss Carlman had to step out into the hall. If we are not studying, we are allowed to whisper a little, if we are not noisy.

"Hey, Annabelle!" I whispered. "What is the deal?"

"You'll find out," Annabelle said.

"If it is worky," Milt said, "the answer is no."

"You can't say no," said Sylvia. "Miss Carlman will not allow it."

Miss Carlman came back and made the announcement. "Now I must talk to the gentlemen. How many of you boys enjoy scout camp? Raise your hands."

We knew it was a trap, but we had to tell the truth, so we raised our hands.

"One hundred per cent," said Miss Carlman. "Well, gentlemen, the girls are Scouts, too, and they enjoy camp as much as you do. So they are going to make Christmas cookies and sell them in the neighborhood, and use the money for their camp fund. However, the cookies will not be very good unless they are fresh, so the girls are going to make them Saturday morning and sell all of them on Saturday afternoon. Annabelle, will you tell them the rest?"

Annabelle stood up and looked around. "We have a perfectly darling idea," she said. "We will all meet at the school at two o'clock on Saturday. Everyone will take five boxes of cookies and sell them, and come back to the school. Then we will have a little party with cookies and cocoa."

"That sounds good, doesn't it?" said Miss Carlman. "How many gentlemen will cooperate? Raise your hands."

I folded my arms across my chest. So did Milt. So did the rest.

"The boys are teasing," Miss Carlman said. "Come, gentlemen, let me see your hands."

We kept our arms folded. Miss Carlman stopped smiling. "Well!" she said. "Will someone please explain? Rupert, what have you to say?"

I stood up. "I am feeling very sad and defeated today," I said. "We had a very sad recess. I am too sad and defeated to say anything cheerful," I sat down.

"Well!" said Miss Carlman. "I must admit I am mystified. Milton, are you defeated and sad, too?"

Milt stood up. "We are all as sad and defeated as Rupert," he said. He wiped his eyes on his wrist, and wiped his wrist on his pants.

Miss Carlman nodded. "That is all very sad, but I am sure you will feel bright and gay after you have had time to think it over. Ready for arithmetic."

After school we met at the "No Dames" corner again.

The girls were standing close by and we talked very loud.

"A fine thing!" said Clayte. "We could be killed in our snow battle, and would Annabelle care? Not Annabelle! Not Sylvia! But now they want to go to Scout camp, so we have to be cooky salesmen."

"It is no disgrace to be a cooky salesman," I said. "But we have to be Girl Scouts, and that is different."

"Very different," said Milt. "I would rather be dead three times!"

"Me, too," said Dood. "Give me liberty or give me death!"

Annabelle moved in. "We have just held a meeting and we wish an explanation," she said. "Why did you refuse to sell our cookies?"

"A very good question," Milt said. "Let me ask you one. Did you see our snow battle this morning?"

Opal began to giggle. "Oh, it was so funny!" she said through her nose. "The way you ran away from those little bits of fifth-graders! Clayte had his jacket pulled over his ears like a turtle, and Milty had a big flat snowball on his head!"

"Very funny!" said Milt. "Ha! Ha! Do you know why the fifth-grade boys with their little fifth-grade muscles could chase us to our corner? Because the fifth-grade women know how to cooperate. They made the snowballs and carried them up to the guys."

"But they're only little girls," said Annabelle, "I mean, we are growing up. We are too old to do such silly, baby things."

"That is how we feel about selling cookies," I said.

The girls did a little whispering. "We are simply too grown up to make your snowballs," Annabelle said. "But we will get the third grade to make them if you will help us sell cookies."

We did a little whispering, too. "Very keen," I said. "Very keen."

"Oh, Rupert!" Annabelle said. "That's wonderful! May we tell Miss Carlman?"

"If you wish," I said.

All the girls were very happy, but they did not know what we had in mind.

"If the third grade is good enough to make our snowballs, the third grade is good enough to sell their cookies," Milt said. "I will talk to my little third-grade cousin, Snooky Morrissey."

Thursday night there was another snowstorm, and Friday morning we built a double fort.

"How about a little battle?" Rick Peterson yelled. He is the biggest fifth-grader. "How would you like to get chased to your corner again?"

We could see the fifth-grade girls making snowballs. They were making them very fast and piling them up, ready to carry to their dear, dear boys.

But we could not say no. It is better to get beaten than to say you are afraid of the fifth grade.

"O.K.," I said. "But we haven't had time to make snowballs. You have girls making yours, and if you are willing to throw the snowballs that girls make, that is all right with us. But you will have to give us some time."

"Five minutes," said Rick.

We made as many snowballs as we could, and we knew that we were going to be defeated again, but that is all in the game.

"O.K.," Rick yelled, "ready or not, the battle is on when I yell 'Go!'" Rick thought he was boss of the playground because the fifth grade had sent us to our corner.

So Rick stood up on a pile of snow and put up his hand with a snowball in it and yelled "Go!" and fired the first shot.

We started throwing as fast as we could, and we could see the fifth-grade girls filling their arms and moving up.

And then we saw something else. A line was moving up behind us from the evergreen hedge. "It's the third grade!" Milt yelled. "That first little peanut is Snooky! A lot of help they'll be!"

Sure enough, it was the third grade, moving up like a line of ants, and they were all carrying snowballs.

"Put 'em down there!" Clayte yelled. "We can use them."

So they began to build a little pile of balls, and we thought it would help a little. But we got a surprise.

The third grade made a sort of circle. They kept coming up and putting down the snowballs and going right back to the evergreen hedge for more.

The line kept moving all the time, and there were so many little ants that they could bring snowballs faster than we could throw them.

The fifth-grade girls could not keep up with us, and in a little while the fifth-grade guys stopped throwing

because they were trying to make their own snowballs.
While they bent over, we kept throwing, so we began
to beat them back.

Soon we chased them onto the safety field where no
one is allowed to play rough, and they were defeated.

When we went in to school, Annabelle said to me,
"I notice you won your snow battle. You must be very
happy."

"Well, I am not so sad," I said.

"The third grade is very loyal to us," Milt said. "I
would rather have the third grade help me than the
sixth-grade girls. The third-graders are smarter and
quicker."

Annabelle flipped her eyelashes. She kind of swal-
lowed and looked at Sylvia. Then they shook their
mittens.

"Well," said Sylvia, "then you will keep your promise
and help us sell our cookies tomorrow?"

"Oh, sure," we said.

And we did. We did not give the job to the third
grade.

It was very easy to sell the cookies. We simply said
to people, "We are Boy Scouts, doing our good deed.
We are selling cookies for the Girl Scouts." We sold
them very fast.

Then we went back for the party. It was keen. Annabelle kept smiling and at last she said, "We know you
were going to send the third grade to sell the cookies.
What made you change your minds?"

"Well," I said, "well . . ."

"I know!" said Sylvia. "It was because the third

grade helped you very well during the snow battle, so you knew that it would only be fair for you to help us. And you know that we are really too grown up to help you fight a snow battle."

"A-hem!" said Milt. "That is part of it. Also those snowballs were better than third-grade snowballs."

"Also," said Clayte, "we noticed that you girls had some very wet mittens to dry after the battle."

"United we stand!" said Dood. And he winked.

So everyone laughed, and Miss Carlman laughed hardest of all, and Annabelle passed the cookies again.

The Birds Take Over

MILT and I were walking to school and day dreaming out loud. I said, "Milt, I saw my first robin this morning. It pushed the memory of snow battles and Girl Scouts and cookies right out of my mind."

"Yes," said Milt, "this is the kind of day to wander out on Highway 41 toward Swedetown Creek."

"I bet the trout are slipping under and over logs in the clear cool water," I said.

Milt kicked a stone and heaved a sigh. "However,

51

dear old Lincoln School calls. Since we smell spring, that means it's almost time for the picnic, which means it's almost time for summer vacation."

I kicked the same stone Milt kicked, and then Dood came running around the corner with Opal and Beautiful Sylvia right behind him.

"So another beautiful day begins," said Milt. Then we all three yelled "Spiders!" Opal shrieked, and Beautiful Sylvia stopped dead in her tracks. We guys got into the sixth-grade room without any trouble.

I looked around the room. It felt different to me. Then I saw them! The walls were covered with pictures of birds.

"What does this mean?" whispered Milt.

Then Miss Carlman said, "I have wonderful news for you. We are going to have a bird club. We will study bird books and learn to know all the birds. To know them is to love them. Rupert, did you say something?"

"Miss Carlman," I said, "isn't a club supposed to be fun?"

"Oh, indeed! We will have lovely hikes in the woods. We will take our bird books along, and when we see a bird, we will find its picture. Won't that be fun?"

On the way home we talked about it. "It is worky," said Dood.

"Correct," Milt agreed. "We have to read all about some dear little birds and give a report. That is worky."

Opal and Beautiful Sylvia and Smart Annabelle were trying to walk with us. "I am very excited," said Opal.

"I am going to study all about orioles tonight so that I can report tomorrow."

"I'm going to study cedar waxwings," Beautiful Sylvia said. "I hope I can find the picture in our bird book."

"Ha," I said. "Cedar waxwings have caps on their heads, and black masks over their eyes, and red spots on their wings. I can show you some in our apple tree. They are beggars."

"Rupert Piper," said Sylvia, "I'm afraid you do not love birds."

"I have to read all about wrens," said Smart Annabelle.

"Wrens!" Milt grinned. "I can tell you what they eat, if you can stand it."

"No, thanks," Annabelle said. "I will get my information from a bird book." And with that the girls turned the corner and left us alone.

We sat on my back porch. "How are your waxwings making out?" Milt asked.

"Well," I said, "it is just work, work, work! Their babies are always hungry. Also, the mother and father sit and talk, and feed each other. I work harder than they do. I am slaving all the time, bringing berries and apples."

"Anyway," Milt said, "they have a keen nest. It has strings from my red sweater and Dood's green one in it."

"They are lucky like my oriole," Dood said. "She has a good soft nest because we had our hair cut and gave her our hair."

The next day Miss Carlman said, "Milton, you will give your report."

"I am pained to report on the cowbird," Milt said. "A cowbird is black, with a brown head. I am sorry to say it is lazy. A cowbird does not build her own nest. She sneaks around and lays her eggs in some smaller bird's nest. But that is not the worst. The cowbird's egg hatches first. The baby cowbird is big and mean. He pushes the other eggs out of the nest. Or else he gets all the food the mother brings because he has the biggest mouth. It is a very sad sight to see a mother sparrow feeding a hungry cowbird that is three times her size."

Smart Annabelle raised her hand. "Miss Carlman, I thought we were learning to love birds, not to gossip about them."

"That's right," Milt said. "I will now sing the cowbird's song."

Milt tipped up his head and began to sing. "Pipe, pipe! Pipe, pipe!"

Opal was next. "Baltimore orioles are very beautiful birds. They build sweet little hanging nests. While the mother sits on the nest, the father oriole sings to her. He sings like this: "Come here, Peter! Come here!"

Opal told us everything she read in the bird book.

"That is a splendid talk about Baltimore orioles," Miss Carlman said.

We studied birds every day, but Miss Carlman said the guys were not becoming bird lovers.

"Birds are too worky," Dood said. "My orioles are out of their nest now, and so are the baby robins. They splash all the water out of the bird bath, and I have to break my back filling it."

"My baby catbirds are pigs," said Clayte. "Very accidentally I found out that they love scrambled eggs, and now I have to go home and scramble one for them." Then he said, "I almost like Mrs. Catbird. She is not very big, but she is scrappy. She can spread out and meow like a cat and scare a blue jay."

That day Miss Carlman told us about the hike. "Our bird club is going to have a hike on Saturday morning." She folded her arms and looked at us boys.

"Oh-oh!" Dood whispered. "Here it comes!"

"I am afraid," Miss Carlman said, "that some of us are not bird lovers, and, of course, do not care to belong to our club, or go on the hike. Ready for recess."

We went down to the "No Dames" corner to talk things over. Dood looked very sad. He said, "It breaks my heart that we are not invited to join the Bird Club and come to school at seven o'clock Saturday morning, and take a long walk to watch our little feathered friends fight."

"That *is* sad," I said.

"Very sad," said Smart Annabelle. The girls had been listening in. "You will miss the breakfast."

This was different. This was news. "What breakfast?" I asked.

"You won't care," said Opal. "It's only orange juice. And pancakes, with all the maple syrup you can eat. And little sausages. You won't care."

"No," said Clayte. "We won't care." He sounded starved.

The girls walked away. "I like birds a little," I said, "but I hate to say so now."

"So do I," said Dood. "Smart Annabelle would say that we just want to join the bird club."

"She would say that we just want to go on the hike," Milt said. "And, of course, that is not true."

"No," I said, "we just want some pancakes and syrup."

"And sausages," Clayte said.

That night there was a very bad storm. Rain poured. The wind howled. My cedar waxwings were safe, sitting in our apple tree which would not blow down.

When Mom woke me up, the sun was shining in my room. Mom said, "I am afraid a lot of nests blew out of trees last night, Rupert."

I went to look in the apple tree. The waxwings' nest was gone.

"I guess it blew away," I said.

"I'm glad those sweet little birds were safely out of it," said Mom, "because you love them so, Rupert."

"I do not," I said. "But I like them, a little."

It was Friday. The girls were excited about the hike, but the boys did not have anything to be excited about.

It was about time to go home, when Miss Carlman said, "Boys, don't forget to meet us at seven o'clock tomorrow."

We were surprised. "Miss Carlman," Dood said, "we did not think we were invited because we complained about the birds' faults."

"Well," said Miss Carlman, "our feathered friends

are not perfect, but we can know all about them and love them just the same."

"But—we did not say we love them," Milt said.

"Oh, well," said Miss Carlman, "some people just study books about birds. Other people feed them and fill their baths."

Then Annabelle had to get smart. "Some people unravel their sweaters, to help make little nests," she said.

"Also," said Beautiful Sylvia, "some people give their hair to the birds."

"The girls brought me something interesting," Miss Carlman said. She reached under her desk and pulled out my waxwings' nest. Then she pulled out Dood's orioles' nest that had Milt's red hair, and Dood's yellow hair, and my curly hair in it. It had some of all the fellows' hair in it.

"I think," Miss Carlman said, "that we have a class of bird lovers. I hope you will all enjoy seeing some beautiful birds tomorrow morning."

"We will also enjoy seeing some beautiful pancakes and syrup and sausages," Milt said.

It was a joke and everyone laughed. Guess who laughed hardest? Miss Carlman!

The Very Queer Ball Game

I MUST say that the bird-club hike was keen, and the breakfast was even keener. But things happened thick and fast in the sixth grade. And before we knew it, it was the last week of school.

"It is time to plan the games and entertainment for our end-of-school picnic," said Miss Carlman.

Sylvia waved. "Miss Carlman, our mothers always work very hard for our picnics. This time, couldn't we girls serve the lunch and let our mothers play? Maybe they would like to play baseball with the boys."

58

"Oh, cute!" said Opal, through her nose.

Very cute. Very ducky. As usual the guys did not have anything to say.

We went down to the "No Dames" corner to talk it over.

"I have a terrible feeling about this picnic," Clayte said. "Suppose a fellow trips someone's mother, or very accidentally hits her with the ball!"

"You know how it is when we let the girls play," I said. "Annabelle makes new rules. One is that you stay batter until you make a home run, and another is that no one can tag you if you've got your fingers crossed. That's how girls play baseball, and mothers are just girls, only older and stiffer."

"This is not a man's world," Clayte said. "And it is not going to be a man's picnic, either."

Well, the picnic day came. My mom was very excited. "I'm taking three dozen sandwiches," she said. "And two cakes. I do hope there is enough to eat. You can't fill boys up!"

"I don't feel hungry," I said. I knew something terrible was going to happen to me that day.

Sure enough, Miss Carlman called me to her. She smiled very sweetly. "Rupert, Annabelle has a very lovely idea, and it is about you."

I know Annabelle. I felt little goose pimples come out on my backbone.

"Please break the news very gently," I said.

Annabelle flipped her eyelashes at me, and Miss Carlman laughed. "Oh, it's not that bad," she said. "In fact, it is an honor, since you have very good eyesight and are very honest. When the boys' team plays baseball with the mothers, you will not play."

"Whoopee!" I said. "Am I ever glad I'm honest and have . . ." Right there I stopped. A very awful thought came to me. "Did you say—good eyesight?"

Annabelle laughed. "Oh, you've guessed the wonderful idea, haven't you, Rupert? You're going to be umpire!"

This hit me. It really hit me. I am a guy who can stand a lot, but I did not think I could stand this. I did not have a chance. Not a chance.

The mothers were very happy to play. Mrs. Snow was ladies' captain, and Clayte Snow was captain of the guys' team.

"We will take the bat and decide who's to bat first," I said.

"Oh, no," said Mrs. Snow. "We will eeny, meeny, miney, mo."

"Well—" I said. I look at the guys. They were all looking at the ground and had their lips stuck out.

"Rupert," said my mom, "be a gentleman!"

"O.K.," I said. I pointed first to Mrs. Snow. I said:

"Eeny, meeny, miney, mo!
Catch a turkey by the toe!
If he hollers, let him go!
Eeny, meeny—"

Right there a terrible thought came to me. The "mo" was going to come out on Clayte, and a gentleman should not bat first.

"Lost my place!" I said. I started on the last "eeny" and made it come out on Mrs. Snow.

She smiled very pretty. "Thank you, Rupert."

So poor old Clayte stepped up to pitch to his mother. First he sent her a curve ball. She swung and missed.

Clayte sent her another. His mom hit it right down the ground so that it bounced three times.

"Strike two!" I yelled.

I could see that Clayte was pretty nervous. But he pitched her a straight ball, and she hit at it, and I don't know how she missed it.

"Strike three! You're out!" I yelled. I was kind of shaking.

"Oh, my!" said Mrs. Snow. "Why didn't you tell me?"

Next, she did a very funny thing. She ran all the bases. And all the while she ran, the other ladies clapped and yelled: "Go, Carrie! Touchdown! Go, Carrie!" And Mrs. Snow waved at them.

There were seven dads present, and they almost died laughing.

When Mrs. Snow got to the home plate she was very happy. "I made it!" she said. "I never thought I would in these shoes. I paid $10.95 for them, but I'd like to make George Seiler take them back!" Then she picked up the bat again.

"Where's that umpire?" some dad yelled.

"Mrs. Snow," I said, "you see, when you're out, you don't bat . . ."

I heard some boos from the ladies.

"Rupert," my mom said, "you be a gentleman!"

So I smiled at Mrs. Snow. "You stand right here," I said. "It is Mrs. Morrissey's turn to bat."

"Oh, excuse me!" said Mrs. Snow. She yelled, "Mrs. Morrissey! Come and bat!"

"Wait till I finish cutting this cake!" Mrs. Morrissey yelled back.

She came, licking her fingers. "Stand here," I said. "Clayte will throw the ball to you. If you hit it, run to first base."

Well she hit it. Then she picked it up and ran to third base and tagged our baseman.

"Oh, no!" I said. "It was a strike. You can bat twice more."

"She's out!" someone yelled.

"Give me the bat," said Mrs. Morrissey.

"You blind, umpire?" the dads yelled.

"Rupert," my mom said, "you be a gentleman."

So I guess it was the first game ever played this way. Mrs. Morrissey batted from third base. Then she batted from second. Then she threw down her bat. "There!" she said. "I'll go back to the cakes. Call me when you need me!"

Miss Smithwick batted next. She is not a mother, but she loves P.T.A. She hit the first ball and was making a home run, but when she got to third, Milt had the ball.

"You're out!" he yelled.

"Milton," his mom said, "is that being a gentleman?"

"She's out!" the dads yelled. "Hey, umpire! You blind?"

"Well . . ." I said.

"Of course I'm out," said Miss Smithwick. "I hope I know the rules of the game."

Doodleberries was up to bat. Mrs. Hall was up to pitch. "Wait till I wind up," she said. She wiggled her arm around some way, and then she picked up the ball and sent it sailing past Dood.

"Ball one!" I yelled.

"Hold your bat straight, Trowbridge," said Mrs. Hall. "How can I hit it when you hold it so slanting?"

Was Dood's face red! She walked him.

"Walk!" I yelled.

I thought the ladies would boo, but they thought it was very cute.

Then Mrs. Hall said it was Mrs. Snows' turn to pitch, and Clayte was up to bat. He made a homer and brought in Doodleberries. But there was trouble.

My mother—my own mother—was shortstop. "You could see," she said, "I was having trouble with my hair when the ball went past me. We'll have to do it over."

Well, if it made her happy—

"Do it over!" I yelled.

So that time Mrs. Morrissey said she would pitch because she wanted to try something. "I've been told," she said, "that one throws better if one looks at something else."

She pitched two wild ones, but Milt hit the third and started to run. Six ladies jumped in from somewhere and covered the ball. Then Mrs. Duncan, who was catcher, got the ball. She held it in both hands and ran the bases, while all the other ladies cheered.

I gave up. Why try to make a baseball game out of this?

"Touchdown!" I yelled. What else would you call it?

"Now, look!" Milt began. "Some umpire! This isn't football!"

"Milton," said Mrs. Morrissey, "be a gentleman. I'm sure Rupert knows a touchdown when he sees one."

So the ladies won the game. We made eight home runs, which counted eight, and the ladies made four touchdowns.

"Four touchdowns count 24," I said. "Everyone knows a touchdown counts six."

"I thought it counted seven," my mom said.

"That's when you make the kick, dear," said Mrs. Morrissey.

I got the idea. I said, "If the ladies had kicked, they surely would have made it. So we will add four more points, and that's 28, and we will give them two more points for being good sports. The ladies win, 30 to eight."

"Lunch time!" said Miss Carlman.

"Man!" my dad said at lunch. "I will have to teach that boy of mine some things."

"I guess he can teach you something about ladies," said Mr. Snow. "Look yonder!"

He pointed at me. I had the biggest dish of ice cream and the biggest piece of cake, and Annabelle was wasting smiles at me.

I thought the guys were mad, but they were not.

"You did your best, Piper," old Milt said. "It was a very queer ball game, and you were a very queer umpire. But you were certainly a gentleman."

Dishpan Hands

WAKEFIELD, and especially the dads, will never forget the queer ball game the moms played with us guys. The best thing about it as far as we're concerned is that it happened on the last day of school. Yes, *sir*, summer vacation is here.

That is, we *thought* it was. But you can count on the girls to mess it up!

"A fine thing!" said Milt. "Our sisters are skipping gaily through the forests and over the beach at dear old Lost Lake, while we stay home doing all their labor."

I said, "I don't mind things like running the vacuum sweeper or tending telephone. But a man's muscles are not made for washing dishes. Also dishwashing is very hard on a man's shoes."

"You are right, Rupert," said Doodleberries. "Look at my shoes—all spattered up with Cheer-O. My hands are raw! Look at them! Wait, I'll wipe them on my pants."

While we were talking, we were very busy scrubbing Clayte Snow's old pig shack, which we were going to make into a very keen kennel for a faithful dog that Clayte was going to win, selling soap.

I mean, it was a pig shack on Mr. Maytag's farm, and then it became a turkey house.

"But I will not keep turkeys any longer," Mr. Maytag said. "They are stupid birds. I built good roosts, but will they roost on them? No! Look at my apple trees! Every one of them full of turkeys! And see that old pig shack? There are maybe ten turkeys in it, huddled together for warmth, this hot summer night! They do everything, and learn everything, the hard way—like some people."

"Well, Mr. Maytag," Clayte said, "I will make a deal with you. I would like to buy the pig shack to make a doghouse."

"I am sorry," Mr. Maytag said, "but that pig shack would make better firewood. A good dog would be ashamed to hang his hat in it."

"I will fix it up," Clayte said.

Mr. Maytag squinted at him. "Seems to me you were

supposed to paint your pa's garage, and he was supposed to give you a dog kennel."

Milt spoke up. Milt is a keen businessman. Milt said: "Anyone can see it is easier to paint the pig shack than to paint a garage. And when you love your dog, you are willing to work for him."

"I see," said Mr. Maytag. "Well, the pig shack is yours if you will take it off my place before sundown tomorrow."

So that was why we were back of Clayte's garage, scrubbing the pig shack and I could hear Ma calling me.

"Rupert! Rupert Piper!"

"She wants to tell me that the sink is full of dishes. Why would I run home to hear stale news like that?" I put some more soap on my scrub brush and scrubbed another board. Dishes are dishes, but a dog is man's best friend.

Then we heard Milt's mother and Doodleberries' mother calling.

Before long all the ladies arrived. They looked at the big shack and looked again.

"What," said Mrs. Snow, "*was* that object?"

"It was a good old pig shack," Clayte said. "I mean, it's a keen kennel."

"Rupert Piper," my mom said, "I'm hoarse from calling you! Annabelle Willman has been phoning, and your dishes are waiting, and—look at you!"

"Mom," I said politely, "I am sorry to say that I can't do dishes. My dishpan hands are too painful. Let me show you. Wait . . ."

"Don't you dare!" Mom said. "Rupert Piper, don't you dare wipe those hands on your pants!"

Then Mrs. Morrissey came, and I could see Smart Annabelle and Beautiful Sylvia coming, too.

"Milton," said Mrs. Morrissey, "if you expect to eat at home, you will immediately come home and wash—wash—eek!" One look at the pig shack made her scream.

Annabelle got there in time to listen in.

"Well," Milt said, "I can see we should put up a "No Dames" sign. He looked right at Annabelle.

Annabelle flipped her eyelashes at him. "I simply came on an errand of mercy," she said. "We are having a perfectly lovely surprise party for Opal Duncan tomorrow, and Sylvia and I came to invite you boys."

At vacation time! Was I mad! "Now, Annabelle!" I said. "Vacation is for fun—not for going to parties or the dentist, or . . ."

"Rupert Piper," said my mom, "you be a gentleman!" Mom smiled at Annabelle. "Rupert will be delighted to attend, dear."

"All the boys will be delighted," Mrs. Snow smiled. Then she gave Clayte a different look. "If you wish to eat at home," she said, "clean up, and wash your dishes."

All of the ladies went away.

"Some vacation!" Milt said in the voice of doom.

We went out on the sidewalk, and Milt bent down and picked up some little pieces of cardboard from the gutter. "Well, you have to eat at home," he said. "Or *do* we?" he exclaimed. "Look, fellows!" Four tickets for dinner at the Northland!"

We read the printing on the tickets:

FOR ELEGANT DINING
HOTEL NORTHLAND
Dinner—Five O'Clock to Midnight
Steak—Chicken—Fish
No Cover Charge

"Free!" said Clayte. "No charge! What time shall we dine?"

"It might look greedy to be the first ones there," I said. "Let's go at ten minutes past five."

So we went home to clean up. My mom was just starting dinner when I came downstairs. She turned white. "Your pink shirt!" she said. "And your bow tie! Rupert Piper, do you mind explaining?"

"It is very simple," I said. "I am simply dining out, elegantly. No dishwashing! So if you will excuse me, dinner is at ten minutes past five. I have spoken. I go."

The telephone was ringing. "Go on, I guess," Mom said. "But I will say one thing. They did not teach me *all* about boys in teacher's college."

She went to answer the phone. I heard her saying: "Rupert, too! I give up! One hour ago, he looked like a swineherd. And now—he is dining out—elegantly!"

The fellows were sitting on the tile step in front of the Northland when I got there. They looked keen. We went inside the hotel, and we could see the dining room. The tables had yellow cloths and little bowls of yellow roses.

Milt said, "Do you all have your tickets?"

We had. So we went in, and a lady came to meet us. She was Mrs. Whittier, who lives near Doodle-berries.

"Well!" she said. "This must be a very special occasion! How would you like this table near the window?"

It was keen. I could see my dad's office across the street.

A waitress came and gave us some menu cards. "We want pie and ice cream," Milt told her.

"But first," I said, "we will have potatoes and gravy and pickles and chicken and stuffing."

"Which vegetable?" said the waitress.

"Pickles will do," I said.

"And which salad?"

"We are not on a diet," Clayte said. "We don't eat salad."

She brought us a tray of celery and olives and radishes, and then she brought us some fruit in a glass dish.

"She is stalling," Milt said. "The chicken isn't done. Maybe it isn't even caught."

But soon she brought the chicken and potatoes and gravy and stuffing.

"Any seconds?" Dood asked her.

She laughed. "You have half a chicken there. You couldn't eat a whole chicken."

"You don't know Dood," we said.

"No," she said, "but I know his mother—and there she is!"

Sure enough, Dood's mom and my mom were driving past. They were going to pick up our dads. They were staring at us as if they were seeing ghosts.

I bowed very politely, and Dood waved his drumstick at them. They opened their eyes wider; but cars began to honk at them, and they had to move on.

After we ate our pie and ice cream we did not wish seconds. "I can still move a little," Milt bragged.

The waitress put a slip of paper beside my plate. It said: "Dinners—four—$10.00."

"Ten dollars," I said. "Boy, are we lucky!"

We took the tickets from our pockets and gave them to the waitress. "We are dining at no charge," I said.

"Oh!" she said. She looked at us. "But—these are only advertising tickets, boys. You will have to pay."

"Ten dollars?" Clayte squeaked. "But . . ."

"I think," the waitress said, "we'd better talk to Mrs. Whittier."

Mrs. Whittier was very nice. "It is a misunderstanding," she said. "Excuse me a moment." Her phone was ringing. We heard a lady's voice. I thought it sounded like Mom.

Mrs. Whittier kept saying: "I see! I see!" When she hung up, she smiled at us. "Boys," she said, "you could help us out a little. Just come with me, please."

She was sort of pushing us along, and in a minute we were in a kitchen, and we were looking at the biggest sink full of necessary evils I ever saw. I mean dirty dishes.

"You wouldn't mind washing a few dishes after such a nice dinner, would you?" Mrs. Whittier said. "Take off your coats. Here are some nice aprons." So we washed the dishes. At eight o'clock there were as many pots and pans as when we started.

"Our moms did this," Milt said.

"You know what?" Clayte said. "I feel like a turkey. We are all like turkeys. We had to do things the hard way, and learn things the hard way. It would have been easier to eat at home and do dishes at home, because at home you get through, some time."

"At home, you get enough pickles," Dood said.

Just then the back door opened and in came Annabelle and Sylvia. "We came to help," Annabelle said.

"Your mothers said you would probably be here until tomorrow, and you would miss Opal's surprise party."

"I'll help wash," said Sylvia.

Dishes are ladies' work, and girls can certainly wash dishes fast.

We are very honest fellows. Milt said, "We wish to thank you. And we will be at Opal's house at two o'clock tomorrow to surprise her. But now, we will go home to bed, as we have had a big evening, and our hands are sore."

When we went outside, a very familiar car was waiting, and my pa was in it. "Pile in, everybody!" he said. "Now! How about being my guest at the ice-cream store for cones or sodas before you go home?"

"That will be very keen," we said.

We all took cones because they do not come in dishes. We did not want to see any more dishes that night.

Pertunias and Onions

EVERYONE knows that it is very hard to get anything to eat in hot weather. Unless, that is, you wash dishes for food. But that is a joke. So I yelled to my mom, "When is dinner?"

"*Dinner!*" Mom said. "Dinner is tonight—I hope! If I don't melt! Lunch was two hours ago. Where were you? Gwen called you a dozen times."

"Well," I said, "how did I know it was lunch time? We hadn't had breakfast yet."

"Rupert Piper," Mom said, "I just wonder if you tell

stories like that to the neighbors! I could not get you up for breakfast. I yanked you and jerked you and simply gave up. You acted like Rip Van Winkle, having his twenty-year nap. Rupert, if you touch that cake . . ."

"A fine thing!" I said. "I am starving—and no cake."

"There's more bread," Mom said. "Or anyway, there will be bread when you run and get some, which I want you to do right now."

"On an empty stomach?"

"Naturally," Mom said. "Unless you'd care for another glass of milk and some more cheese and ham and cookies and hard boiled eggs."

"What?" I said. "No pickles?"

But the telephone rang, and Mom went to answer.

I was finishing a cold egg when she came back and looked at me. "That was Miss Smithwick," she said, in the voice of doom.

I gave her a big smile. "How is Miss Smithwick?" I asked.

"Never mind that. When did you see her?" Mom said.

"Yesterday," I said. "Do you see this ear? Well, Miss Smithwick's fingerprints are on it. She held me by this ear, and asked me if I had been running through her pertunias."

"Petunias," Mom corrected me. "Tell me some more."

"I said, 'No, Miss Smithwick, I have not seen your beautiful pertunias all summer, and you will notice that the footprints are lots bigger than a sixth-grader can make.'"

"What did she say to that?" Mom asked.

"She said, "Rupert, the word is *petunia*.'"

"We are wasting time," Mom said. "Rupert Piper, someone has pulled all Miss Smithwick's onions!"

"Well," I said, "can I help that?"

"I wonder," she said. "When you came home last night, you had been eating onions."

"I am very, very hurt," I said. "Give me a quarter, Ma, and I will go and get the bread."

"Rupert Piper," Mom said, "you sit right smack on this kitchen stool and tell me whether you boys pulled Miss Smithwick's onions."

"We did not," I said. "Mom, I am telling you the truth."

"Then, where did you get the onions you ate?"

"It is a very sad story," I said. "It will break your heart."

"I will risk that," she said. "Start talking."

"All the guys were starved yesterday," I said. "Milt's mother told him to keep out of the icebox, or else! Doodleberries' mother is painting her kitchen and is very cross, and all their crackers taste of paint. And poor old Clayte—I don't think you can take this, Mom."

"Try me," she said.

"Well, poor Clayte has not had one bite to eat this week."

Mom looked at me.

"At the table, that is," I said. "But Clayte would rather starve and be a cold, lifeless form than to sneak down the alley in the night and steal onions from Miss Smithwick's dear little pertunia bed."

"*Petunia*," Mom said. "And you haven't mentioned where you got the onions."

"Even a starving man has a right to some secrets," I said. "But you can figure it out for yourself. There is a farmers' market in Laney's vacant lot—every Thursday. There are a few vegetables that are spotty and wilted and beat up and do not sell. So when the kindhearted farmers see some people's poor, scrubby, starving boys—well, figure it out, Ma."

"H'm!" said Mom. "Well, go get the bread, Rupert. I read a library full of books on how to raise boys—but those writers had not met Rupert Piper." Mom went to the telephone.

All the guys had to go to the store, so I had news for them. "You know," I said, "when we saw Bill Andrews and Chuck Files and Fritz Craig bustling out of Miss Smithwick's alley, last night? Well, all Miss Smithwick's onions got pulled. And guess who got the credit! Us!"

"She called my mom, too," Milt said. "She didn't exactly blame us."

"She just wondered about us," Dood said. "My mom got very excited."

"Mine, too," Clayte said. "I had to tell her about the farmers' market."

"We can't tell on Bill and Chuck and Fritz," I said. "They are ninth-graders and twice as big as we are."

"We are not afraid, but guys with brains do not mix with musclemen like Bill and Chuck and Fritz."

"They are always running through Miss Smithwick's pertunias," Dood said.

"Well," Milt said, "let's take our bread home, and then see if we can find something to eat somewhere. I have not had anything to eat today."

"Neither have I," I said.

"So we took our bread and things home, and then went to the bakery. "Stand there and look at the pies in the window," Milt said.

"The cupcakes look better," I said. "You need a fork to eat pie."

"I don't," said Clayte. "The cavemen didn't have forks."

Then we went in. Milt talked. The rest of us looked at the cupcakes. "Mrs. Miller," Milt said in a very hungry voice, "we are wondering if you have a little work for us."

"I certainly have!" Mrs. Miller said.

We took our hands out of our pockets and got ready.

"My delivery boy hasn't shown up," Mrs. Miller said. "I baked for Mrs. Armstrong's and Mrs. Swanson's parties, and I have promised sixteen other deliveries."

So Milt and I made three trips to Mrs. Armstrong's house, and Clayte and Dood made three to Mrs. Swanson's. Then we each made four trips to other people's houses. We started at three o'clock, and it was only half past four when we were through.

"Thank you so much!" Mrs. Miller said.

"We were very glad to help," Milt said. "Even if we were hungry." We looked at the cupcakes.

But Mrs. Miller was opening her money drawer. "How about thirty cents apiece?" she said.

Our teeth almost dropped out. We were not thinking

of money. We were just thinking of a smart, easy way to get a free cupcake.

"It's a deal!" Clayte said. Then he remembered his manners. "I mean, thirty cents will be very nice, thank you."

"And won't you have some cupcakes?" Mrs. Miller said.

So we each got thirty cents and two cupcakes.

When we went outside who should be across the street, looking hungry, but Smart Annabelle, Beautiful Sylvia, and Opal.

"Creeps!" Milt said. "Those women! They know we have money in our wallets and cupcakes in this bag."

"Hi, Rupert!" Annabelle called. "Isn't it warm?" She was wasting smiles on me, way across the street.

"I saw her at nine o'clock, and at ten, and eleven," I said. "I saw her at one o'clock, and two, and every time I told her it was warm."

Clayte yelled at her. "Boo-oo! We are freezing to death!"

Opal giggled. "Oh, Claytie! You're so cute!" she said.

"I wish we were going for ice cream," Sylvia said. "Like you boys." So that was why we climbed the elm tree. The elm tree is practically a "No Dames" corner because the girls cannot climb it.

They stood under it, and Annabelle giggled. "You look like turkeys roosting up there," she said.

"You look like raccoons," Sylvia said.

Then Opal howled, like a coon dog. She only did it for fun, and soon they went away.

So we were up there, eating our cupcakes in peace,

when we saw Bill and Chuck and Fritz coming down the street. They did not see us.

Bill said, "Don't turn down Miss Smithwick's alley. It's still daylight."

Chuck said, "She sure was mad about her onions! She can't take a joke. If my mom knew I helped pull the onions, I sure would catch it!"

Fritz said, "Let's have some more fun tonight. When we come home from the Western, let's pull all those flowers."

So they went along, and Milt said, "Oh-oh! Tomorrow we will be in Dutch again."

"They are mean guys," I said. "We ought to tell Miss Smithwick."

"Who wants to get beat up?" Clayte said. "Not me!"

"Just the same," Milt said, "we ought to tell."

"We could ask Miss Smithwick not to tell who told her," Dood said.

"Never trust a woman," Clayte said. "She will forget and tell."

But Miss Smithwick is a very keen lady. We felt very sorry for her. She is very proud if she can keep her flowers blooming until the snow comes.

"Let's send her a note," Dood said. "I've got a stamp in my wallet. Look."

I said, "A stamp is no good when you have used it to wrap gum."

"Anyway, she wouldn't get it until tomorrow," Milt said. "Her pertunias will be dead and departed."

We could hardly eat our cupcakes because we felt so sorry for Miss Smithwick.

When I went home, there was no one near the telephone, so I dialed Miss Smithwick's number.

"This is a friend," I said. "Watch your pertunia bed after the Western tonight." Then I hung up. My heart was pounding.

I did not tell a soul. I did not even tell the guys.

Well, we noticed that Bill and Chuck and Fritz got a job for the rest of the summer. They had to weed and water Miss Smithwick's garden, and mow her lawn, and trim her hedge and things.

One day they met Ruthie Carter on the street. She is as big as my sister Gwen. Ruthie wasted smiles on them.

"I imagine you're going to make lots of money this summer," she said.

"Well," Chuck said, "to tell you the truth, we took our pay in onions." He winked at Bill and Fritz. Then he grabbed his back, and moaned. "Oh, my aching back!"

I went home and Mom said, "Rupert, there is a package on the desk for you."

It was a box of candy. There was a note. It read: "To a Friend: The word is PETUNIA. M. Smithwick."

Milt and Clayte and Dood had candy and notes. The notes were just like mine. So I knew they had phoned Miss Smithwick, too.

After supper I passed my candy. "It's very good," Mom said. "But I don't understand why Miss Smithwick did it."

"That's easy," I said. "Miss Smithwick knows that boys have a very hard time getting something to eat in hot weather. Have another piece!"

Fishing Trip

CLOVER LAKE is a very keen lake with some very keen cottages where we go for three weeks every summer. Clayte and his mom and dad go, too. The only trouble with this very keen spot is that Smart Annabelle's mom and dad also go along, and, naturally, that means that Annabelle goes right along with them! Clover Lake should *not* be for girls!

Well, Clayte and I were climbing into our rowboat for a very peaceful morning of fishing when up comes Smart Annabelle. "I want to go fishing with you," she said.

"Now look, Annabelle," Clayte said. "We took you fishing last year and what happened? Your yakety-yak kept the big ones scared away."

"Also, I said, "you made paper boats and swam them around."

"Rupert, I caught lots of fish!"

"Minnies," I said. "All perch, three or four inches long! You filled the boat with those things, and Clayte and I had to row 'em in and then dump them back!"

"But, Rupert, I've been studying fishing magazines all year!"

"You have a very wonderful brain, Annabelle," Clayte said like a smoothie. "Very wonderful—for arithmetic and history. But you don't catch fish with books."

"But, Clayton . . ."

Clayte came to the point. "The subject is closed. This is strictly a man's fishing trip. No girls are invited."

"I agree with Clayte," I said.

"But, Rupert," Annabelle said, "I simply love to fish, and the only chance I have to fish is when someone with big muscles like yours goes along to row."

She was buttering me up. I know Annabelle!

Just then Mom stuck her head out our cottage window. "Rupert Piper, where are you manners?" she inquired. "Certainly you boys are going to take Annabelle fishing. Now let's not hear another word about it."

I could see that we were outtalked, but I had an idea. I turned up the corners of my mouth and showed

Annabelle all my teeth so that she'd think I was smiling at her.

"O.K., Annabelle," I said. "We'll let you know what time. C'mon and dig worms, Clayte. We'll dig some fat ones for you, Annabelle."

Clayte looked at me as if he thought I was crazy.

We went down the beach and went back of the boathouse to dig. Clayte said, "You grinned at Annabelle like some old movie actor."

"Look," I said, "you know what time we're going fishing? Five a.m.! Right when Smart Annabelle is very busy getting her beauty sleep!"

Clayte held out his hand. "You're a genius, Piper," he said. "A genius. Shake on it!"

I shook.

Before noon Mom sent me to the grocery and I found out the news. There was going to be a fishing derby in the morning for everyone under fifteen, with prizes for the biggest fish of each kind. Swell prizes like a casting rod and a Kodak. There were sissy prizes, too, for girls.

"If they give a prize for the smallest fish, Annabelle will win it," I said.

"Not in our boat!" Clayte told me.

Before supper Annabelle was down on the beach when we went for our swim.

"Oh, Rupert," she said, "What time are we going?"

"Five o'clock," I said.

"O.K."

"I mean five in the morning, natch," I said, and waited for Annabelle to faint in the sand.

"O.K. Rupert," she said. "I'll be ready."

"Like fun!" I said.

I set our alarm for a quarter to five. It went off like a siren. I figured I could get dressed in five minutes, so I just shut my eyes again. I wasn't asleep—just had my eyes shut—when, all of a sudden, I heard a whooping outside my window. First I thought it was cats fighting. But I looked out and there was Annabelle ready to go fishing, with a rod over her shoulder and a creel on her arm.

"Ready, Rupert?" she yelled.

I groaned.

While I got dressed, I heard Annabelle whooping under Clayte's window.

Old Clayte was very glum on the way down to the water. He put one foot on the boat and made a speech to Annabelle.

"O.K., Annabelle, we're being kind enough to take you fishing. But there are some rules you won't find in books. First, you are not to speak one word from the time we shove off until we make port."

Annabelle smiled. "That's ducky, Clayton. I like to be quiet when I fish."

"Second rule," said Clayte, "you will bait your own hook."

"Oh, sure," said Annabelle.

"Third rule," said Clayte, "you will remove your fish from the hook without help."

She smiled. "I've studied that, too."

"Fourth and last rule," said Clayte, "You will immediately throw back everything you catch.

There are times when I am really proud to know Clayte. This was one of those times.

Annabelle stopped smiling. "But, Clayton . . ."

"I agree with Clayte," I said. "We do not wish to row a ton of minnies around."

"But suppose I catch a big one! I might win the derby. Besides, I've studied so hard."

"Rules are rules," I said.

Clayte glared at her. "Throw back everything you catch even if it's Jonah and the whale! Promise, or you don't go!"

"I promise," said Annabelle.

We put Annabelle in the middle of the boat where we could keep an eye on her. I took the oars.

The lake isn't very deep and there were other boats out, so we felt safe. Even if we tipped over, we'd only get soaked.

We went out a distance, dropped the anchor, and began to fish.

First thing, Annabelle got a bite. She flipped a shiner up in the air and brought it in, wiggling like some goldfish. She looked kind of sly as if she'd like to slip it in her pocket or something. But she could feel a pair of very cold eyes boring into her from two directions. She slipped Mr. Shiner from the hook, tossed him back, and looked very sadly after him.

Clayte and I grinned at each other. That was when I lost the big bass.

"Nothing but a big bass would bite so hard, and get away so fast, because I wasn't looking," I said to Clayte.

"It's Annabelle's fault," Clayte said over her head. "Always monkeying with shiners."

Just then she caught another, a monster, all of three inches long. A sea gull watched her toss it back and flopped down and grabbed it. Then he sat on the water and watched Annabelle very fondly.

"I guess he made up his sea-gull mind he's going to get a free breakfast," Clayte said. "This is very embarrassing."

"It's Annabelle's fault," I said.

Just then my line gave a tug, but I was too late. I thought I saw a big pickerel swim off. Annabelle's fault!

We moved over to a different spot. Our luck was the same, but Annabelle hauled in a bass. It looked about five inches long—a short five inches. She patted it and stretched it. But Clayte and I kept giving her some cold looks until she tossed it to her gull.

She caught some more bass and tossed them back. Two more gulls came.

I caught a bass. It was about five inches—a long five inches. I decided to toss it back later.

While I was baiting my hook, I noticed Annabelle taking something from her pocket and putting it in her mouth. Very impolite!

In a minute she flipped her line over. I saw it jerk, and up came a trout fourteen inches long. Well, a short fourteen inches! While we watched, Annabelle flipped it overboard.

I felt a good tug at my line and saw a sunfish swim

off. When I looked again, Annabelle was hauling out a sunfish—a whopper. It should have been mine.

Annabelle tossed it back.

"What are you eating, Annabelle?" Clayte said. "You may speak."

"Oh, nothing."

Very impolite!

"You've got five gulls waiting around for your fish," I said. "I'd rather have paper boats."

Just then Annabelle landed a big black bass that would scare you. I felt a little sad, seeing it go back in the water. Annabelle was very quiet.

Then Clayte had an idea. "Annabelle," he said, "since you came uninvited, and since you can't row, and since your gulls scare our catch away, I suggest you bait our hooks. Especially since you've read a book."

Annabelle never said a word. She baited Clayte's hook and tossed it in—then mine. In a minute, I landed a bass as big as a cow. Well, a small cow.

Clayte whistled. "Nice little bass, Piper."

"Thanks," I said.

Annabelle went right on chewing whatever was in her pocket. I tossed my line at her. She baited the hook and tossed it in, and wasted a smile on me.

Right then Clayte got a bite that shook the boat. He made a big fuss landing the fish.

"A very fair-sized bass," I said. "Very fair, for a guy your age."

"Thanks," said Clayte. "It's nothing. It's only an inch bigger than yours."

Annabelle went on chewing. While she baited Clayte's hook and tossed it in, I brought out a trout.

"Wow!" Clayte said. "Some trout, boy!"

"Of course," I said. "I'm a real fisherman when I get started."

Annabelle kind of choked on what she was chewing.

I slipped my trout off the hook. "Hey!" I said. "Annabelle Willman, what's this stuff you're baiting our hooks with?"

"Yeah," said Clayte. "I just remembered, you don't have any worms. You are now permitted to speak."

Annabelle looked very innocent. "Why, I've simply been baiting them the way it says in my book, with good old paraffin."

"Paraffin!" I said. "But how . . ."

Annabelle took something out of her mouth and held it up. It looked like a pearl, or like a tiny egg in the light.

"You roll it into a ball in your mouth—it says in the book," said Annabelle.

Just then someone whooped from shore. It was Clayte's dad. "Breakfast! Last call. You kids get in here!"

We took our catch to the sporting-goods store and had it weighed in. In the evening, everyone went down for the announcement of prizes. Mr. Fifield was master of ceremonies."

Clayte's bass won a prize.

"But the grand prize goes to a young fisherman, Mr. Rupert Piper, for a trout that's the envy of all us an-

glers. Care to tell us what you used, Rupert?" Mr. Fifield looked very coy.

I'd rather be dead three times, I thought. I'd rather
not get the prize. I'd rather be dead.

Clayte felt the same.

"Not telling?" Mr. Fifield said. "Well, that's all
right. You don't have to give away any secrets. The
prizes are this beautiful Shakespeare reel, or this ex-
quisite gold compact. Which will you take, Rupert?
As if I didn't know!" He was reaching the reel toward
me.

"I'll take the compact," I moaned.

Mr. Fifield smiled. "Oh, for your mother!"

Later, on the way home, Clayte asked, "What's the
idea, taking an old compact?"

"Well," I said, "It's this way." Suddenly it came to
me. "Smart Annabelle isn't so dumb. If she hadn't
learned to chew paraffin, we'd never have caught those
fish. So she really deserves the compact."

"Uh," grunted Clayte.

"And furthermore," I said, "in two weeks we'll be in
the seventh grade. Who knows how dead that will be.
You've got to admit that Annabelle adds a little spice
to our sometimes sad existence."

Clayte just looked at me and shook his head. "I'd
rather be dead three times," he said. "I begin to see
the end. The 'No Dames' corner? I can see it now.
It'll be known as the 'Dames Invited' corner. You have
my sympathy, Piper."

"Cheer up," I said. "There's still Beautiful Sylvia and
Opal." Then I ran!